# minedition

English edition published 2016 by Michael Neugebauer Publishing Ltd. Hong Kong

Text and Illustration copyright © 2016 Nikolai Popov
Rights arranged with "minedition" Rights and Licensing AG, Zurich, Switzerland.

Michael Neugebauer Publishing Ltd., Unit 23, 7F, Kowloon Bay Industrial Centre,
15 Wang Hoi Road, Kowloon Bay, Hong Kong. Phone 852 2807 1711,
e-mail: info minedition.com
This edition was printed in July 2016 at L.Rex Printing Co Ltd.
3/F., Blue Box Factory Building, 25 Hing Wo Street, Tin Wan, Aberdeen,
Hong Kong, China
Typesetting in Bradley Hand ITC
Color separations by Pixelstorm, Vienna.
Library of Congress Cataloging-in-Publication Data available upon request.

ISBN 978-988-8341-31-3

10 9 8 7 6 5 4 3 2 1
First impression

For more information please visit our website: www.minedition.com

# Kwik & Kwak

Nikolai Popov

## Never Give Up

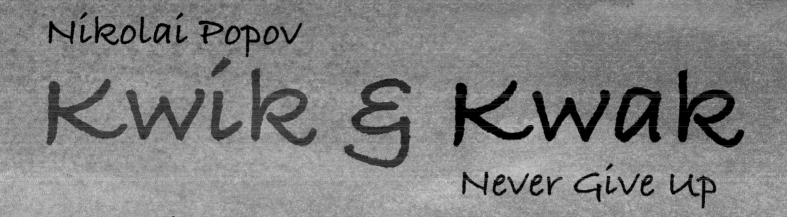

minedition

There is absolutely nothing to do.

Come on, let's have an adventure!

But it looks dangerous out here...

... You see, I told you!

Don't give up. There's always another way.

Let's try to make things better.

Look at how smoothly we can go!

I knew we should have slowed down.

How about we try again with something else?

Now we're on our way.

Hang on, this storm is too much!

Where did you go?

Over here. I'm all tangled up. And I am cold!

Finally everything is perfect.

Whoa! I told you this was a bad idea!

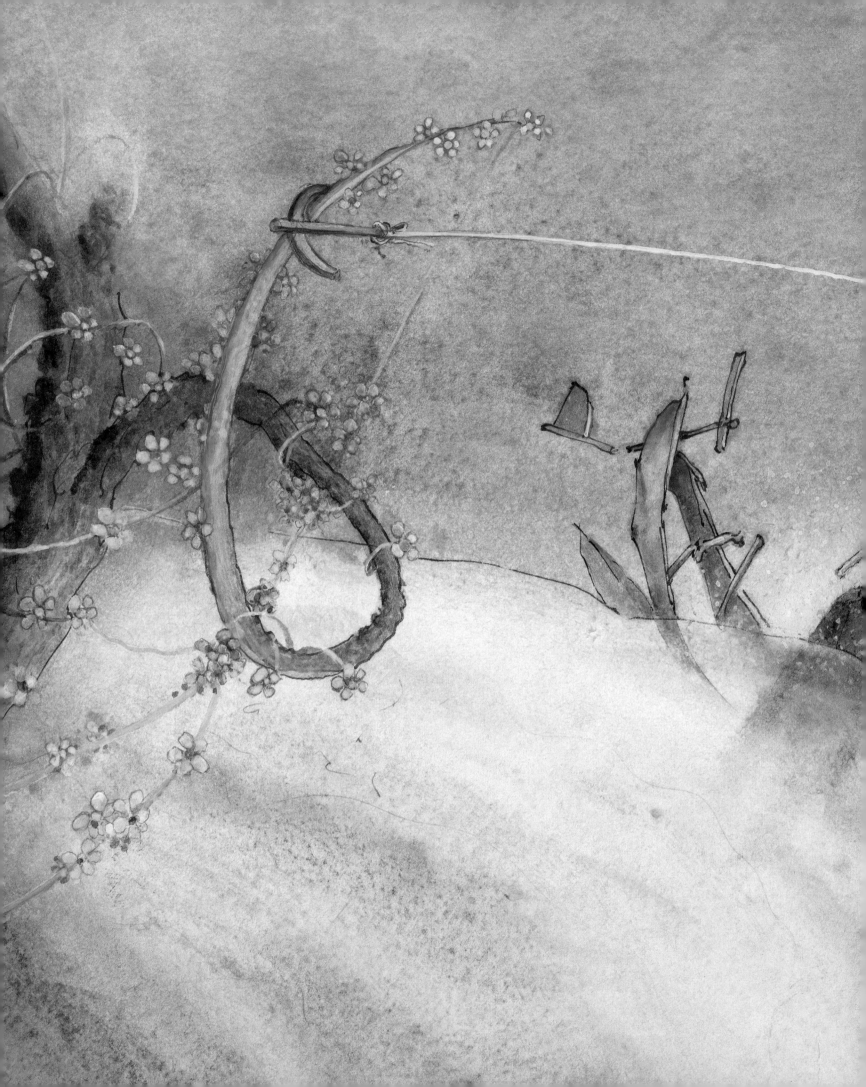

Just have a little faith.

Never give up...

And we'll both be okay.